ISABELLA
OR·THE·POT
OF·BASIL

后浪 | 插 图 珍 藏 版

伊莎贝拉

[英]
约翰·济慈
著

[英]
威廉·布朗·麦克杜格尔
绘

朱维基
译

江苏凤凰文艺出版社
JIANGSU PHOENIX LITERATURE AND
ART PUBLISHING

1

美丽的伊莎贝拉，天真可怜的伊莎贝拉！

　罗伦索，爱神眼中的年轻朝拜者！

他们同住在一座院子里，

　怎能不心动，不患一些病痛；

他们同桌进餐怎能不感到

　互相偎依在一起是多大的安慰；

当然啰，他们在同一个屋顶下睡眠，

怎能不互相做梦，怎能不每夜流泪。

1

Fair Isabel, poor simple Isabel!

　　Lorenzo, a young palmer in Love's eye!

They could not in the self-same mansion dwell

　　Without some stir of heart, some malady;

They could not sit at meals but feel how well

　　It soothed each to be the other by;

They could not, sure, beneath the same roof sleep

But to each other dream, and nightly weep.

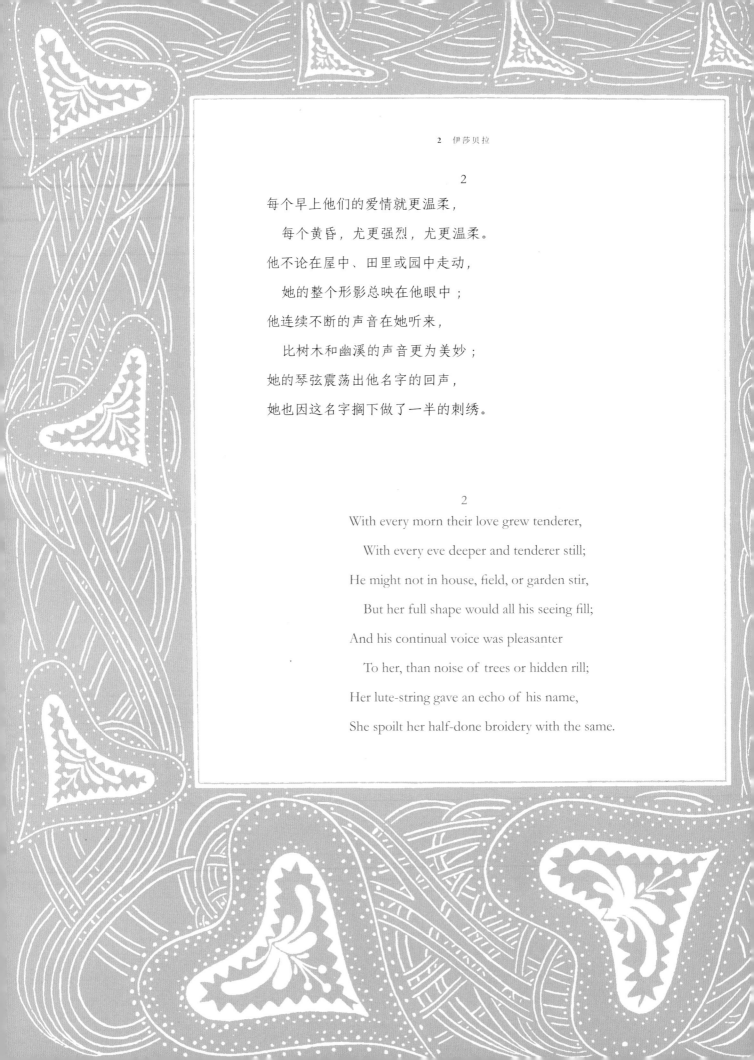

2

每个早上他们的爱情就更温柔，

　　每个黄昏，尤更强烈，尤更温柔。

他不论在屋中、田里或园中走动，

　　她的整个形影总映在他眼中；

他连续不断的声音在她听来，

　　比树木和幽溪的声音更为美妙；

她的琴弦震荡出他名字的回声，

她也因这名字搁下做了一半的刺绣。

2

With every morn their love grew tenderer,

　　With every eve deeper and tenderer still;

He might not in house, field, or garden stir,

　　But her full shape would all his seeing fill;

And his continual voice was pleasanter

　　To her, than noise of trees or hidden rill;

Her lute-string gave an echo of his name,

She spoilt her half-done broidery with the same.

3

他知道谁的纤手放在门闩上，

　　用不着门儿送她映入眼帘；

他从她卧室的窗看见她的美色，

　　能比猎鹰的眼睛窥探得更远；

他会守望得像她晚祷那样恒久，

　　因为她的脸仰望同一的天堂；

通夜消磨在痛苦的相思中，

要听她早晨下楼的脚步声。

3

He knew whose gentle hand was at the latch,

　　Before the door had given her to his eyes;

And from her chamber-window he would catch

　　Her beauty farther than the falcon spies;

And constant as her vespers would he watch,

　　Because her face was turn'd to the same skies;

And with sick longing all the night outwear,

To hear her morning-step upon the stair.

4

整个长长的五月处在这悲切境地中，

　　到了六月初他们的面颊更惨白：

"明天我要向我的丽人俯首折腰，

　　明天我要向我的情人恳求恩赐。"——

"罗伦索啊，你的嘴唇若不唱出

　　相思的曲调，我就在今夜死去。"——

他们就这样各自向枕头低诉；但是，唉，

他们却让无情无义的日子一天天流去！

4

A whole long month of May in this sad plight

　　Made their cheeks paler by the break of June:

"To-morrow will I bow to my delight,

　　To-morrow will I ask my lady's boon." —

"O may I never see another night,

　　Lorenzo, if thy lips breathe not love's tune." —

So spake they to their pillows; but, alas,

Honeyless days and days did he let pass;

5

可爱的伊莎贝拉未被碰过的面颊，

　　那应当有红晕的地方却变得苍白了，

瘦成个要用声声抚慰

　　减轻婴孩痛苦的年轻母亲的脸：

"她病得多厉害啊！"他说，"我不能说，

　　可是我想说，把我的相思和盘托出：

若是容貌能表达衷情，我要喝她的泪，

这样至少会吓走她心中的忧虑。"

5

Until sweet Isabella's untouch'd cheek

　　Fell sick within the rose's just domain,

Fell thin as a young mother's, who doth seek

　　By every lull to cool her infant's pain:

"How ill she is," said he, "I may not speak,

　　And yet I will, and tell my love all plain:

If looks speak love-laws, I will drink her tears,

And at the least 'twill startle off her cares."

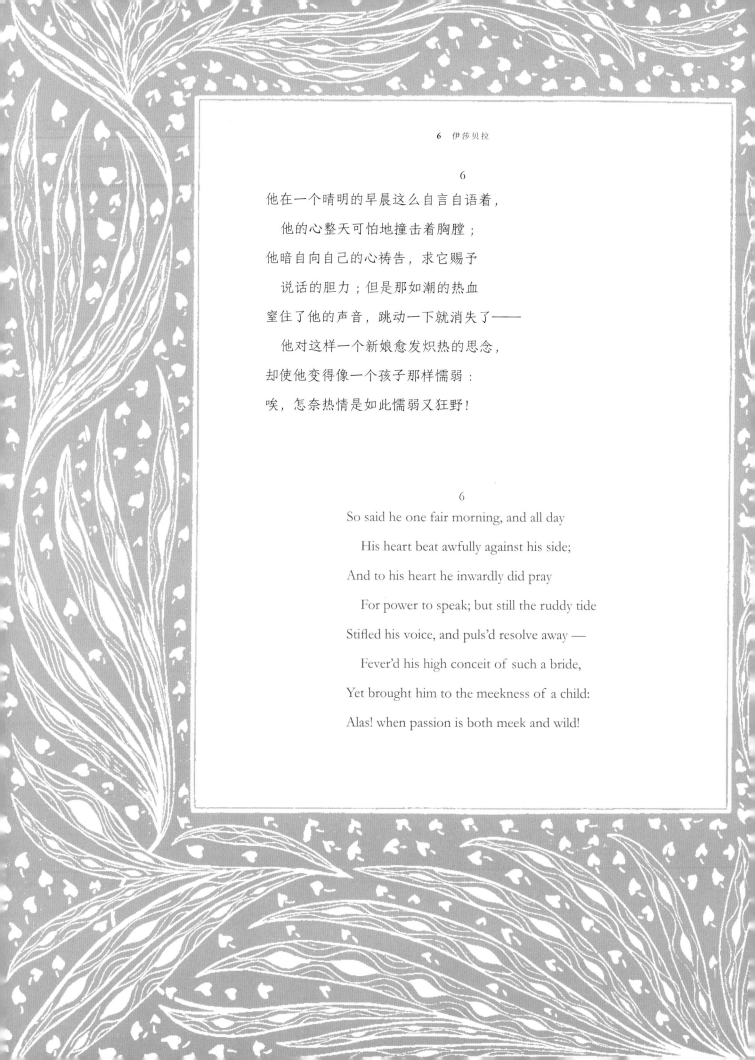

6

他在一个晴明的早晨这么自言自语着，

　　他的心整天可怕地撞击着胸膛；

他暗自向自己的心祷告，求它赐予

　　说话的胆力；但是那如潮的热血

窒住了他的声音，跳动一下就消失了——

　　他对这样一个新娘愈发炽热的思念，

却使他变得像一个孩子那样懦弱：

唉，怎奈热情是如此懦弱又狂野！

6

So said he one fair morning, and all day

　　His heart beat awfully against his side;

And to his heart he inwardly did pray

　　For power to speak; but still the ruddy tide

Stifled his voice, and puls'd resolve away —

　　Fever'd his high conceit of such a bride,

Yet brought him to the meekness of a child:

Alas! when passion is both meek and wild!

7

因此伊莎贝拉那双敏捷的眼睛

　　若看不出他高高额头上的每个迹象；

他又会再次醒来痛苦地度过

　　一个充满相思和悲哀的凄凉夜晚，

她看到那额头十分苍白阴沉，

　　立刻满脸通红；因此温柔地叫道，

"罗伦索！"这会儿她虽不作胆怯地询问，

他却从她的声音和表情中明白了一切。

7

So once more he had wak'd and anguished

　　A dreary night of love and misery,

If Isabel's quick eye had not been wed

　　To every symbol on his forehead high;

She saw it waxing very pale and dead,

　　And straight all flush'd; so, lisped tenderly,

"Lorenzo!" —here she ceas'd her timid quest,

But in her tone and look he read the rest.

8

"伊莎贝拉啊！我心中能一半感到，

　　可以悄悄地向你说出我的苦楚；

倘若你以前曾相信过任何事情，

　　请相信我如何爱你，相信我的灵魂

如何临近它的劫数：我决不用

　　不受欢迎的紧握使你的手疼痛，

决不用凝望使你的眼睛惊惶；

但我不能再活一夜，倘若无法倾诉热情与衷肠。

8

"O Isabella, I can half perceive

　　That I may speak my grief into thine ear;

If thou didst ever any thing believe,

　　Believe how I love thee, believe how near

My soul is to its doom: I would not grieve

　　Thy hand by unwelcome pressing, would not fear

Thine eyes by gazing; but I cannot live

Another night, and not my passion shrive.

9

"爱人啊！你引我离开冬天的寒冷，

　　情人啊！你引我走向夏天的热浪，

我一定要品尝在这个恩情深厚的早晨里，

　　在这孕育成熟的暖意中绽开的花朵。"

这么说着，他先前怯弱的嘴唇大胆了起来，

　　用如露的音韵和她的嘴唇一起吟咏：

他们感到无上的福佑，无比的幸福

就像是在六月阳光中盛开的花朵。

9

"Love! thou art leading me from wintry cold,

　　Lady! thou leadest me to summer clime,

And I must taste the blossoms that unfold

　　In its ripe warmth this gracious morning time."

So said, his erewhile timid lips grew bold,

　　And poesied with hers in dewy rhyme:

Great bliss was with them, and great happiness

Grew, like a lusty flower in June's caress.

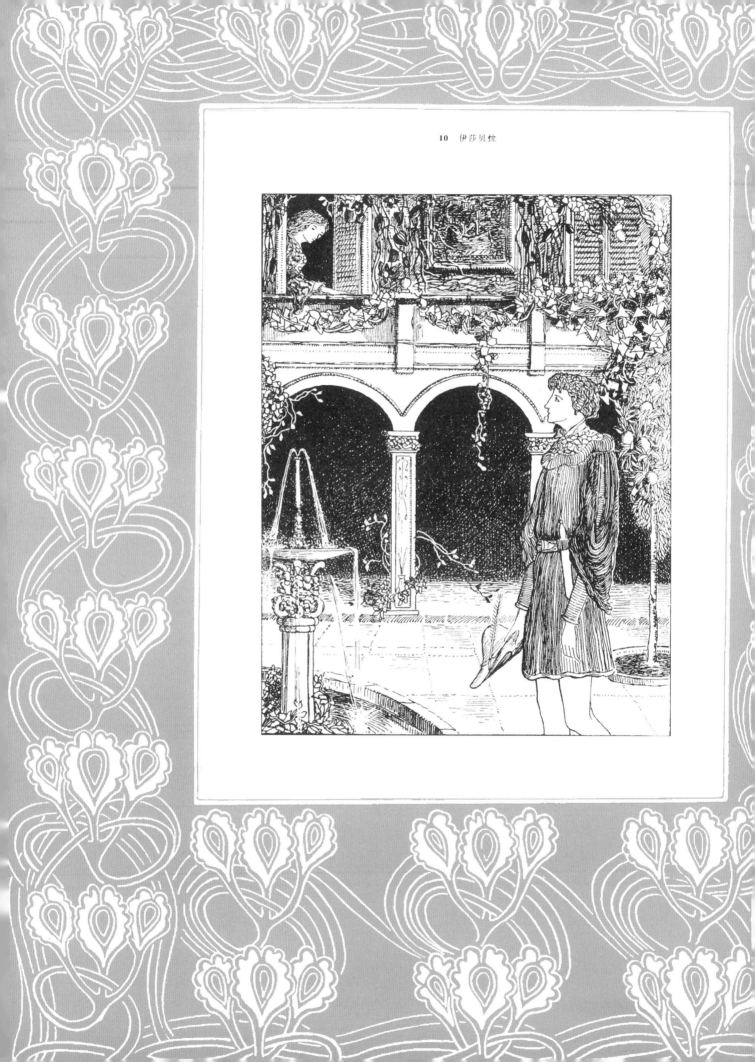

10

他们俩似乎欢天喜地地分手，

　　像并蒂的两朵玫瑰给微风吹开

只是为了能更亲密地再次合拢，

　　共享各自心里隐藏的芬芳。

她走到自己的闺房，唱支美妙的歌，

　　唱的是缠绵的相思和甜蜜的情意；

他以轻快的脚步走上西边的一座山丘，

向太阳依依辞别，心中充满欢畅。

10

Parting they seem'd to tread upon the air,

　　Twin roses by the zephyr blown apart

Only to meet again more close, and share

　　The inward fragrance of each other's heart.

She, to her chamber gone, a ditty fair

　　Sang, of delicious love and honey'd dart;

He with light steps went up a western hill,

And bade the sun farewell, and joy'd his fill.

11

他们又暗暗相会，那时薄暮

　　还未揭去蒙在群星上的美丽面纱，

他们每到黄昏就暗暗相会，那时薄暮

　　还未揭去蒙在群星上的美丽面纱，

暗暗地在一个种着风信子和麝香花的花亭里，

　　无人知道，也听不到任何人的窃窃私语。

唉！但愿他们能永远像这样在一起，

永不要有闲人的耳朵以他们的悲痛为乐。

11

All close they met again, before the dusk

　　Had taken from the stars its pleasant veil,

All close they met, all eves, before the dusk

　　Had taken from the stars its pleasant veil,

Close in a bower of hyacinth and musk,

　　Unknown of any, free from whispering tale.

Ah! better had it been for ever so,

Than idle ears should pleasure in their woe.

12

那他们是不幸福吗? ——决不可能——

　　他们俩已为彼此落下太多的眼泪,

我们已用太多的喟叹酬报他们,

　　他们死后我们已寄予太多的同情,

我们的确见过太多的悲惨故事,

　　那些事迹都应被雕刻在灿烂的黄金上传于后世;

除了讲到忒修斯[1]的妻子如何隔着

不可渡越的大海向他遥拜的故事。

12

Were they unhappy then? — It cannot be —

　　Too many tears for lovers have been shed,

Too many sighs give we to them in fee,

　　Too much of pity after they are dead,

Too many doleful stories do we see,

　　Whose matter in bright gold were best be read;

Except in such a page where Theseus' spouse

Over the pathless waves towards him bows.

---

1 希腊神话中的雅典王子,曾进入克里特迷宫斩妖除怪的英雄。

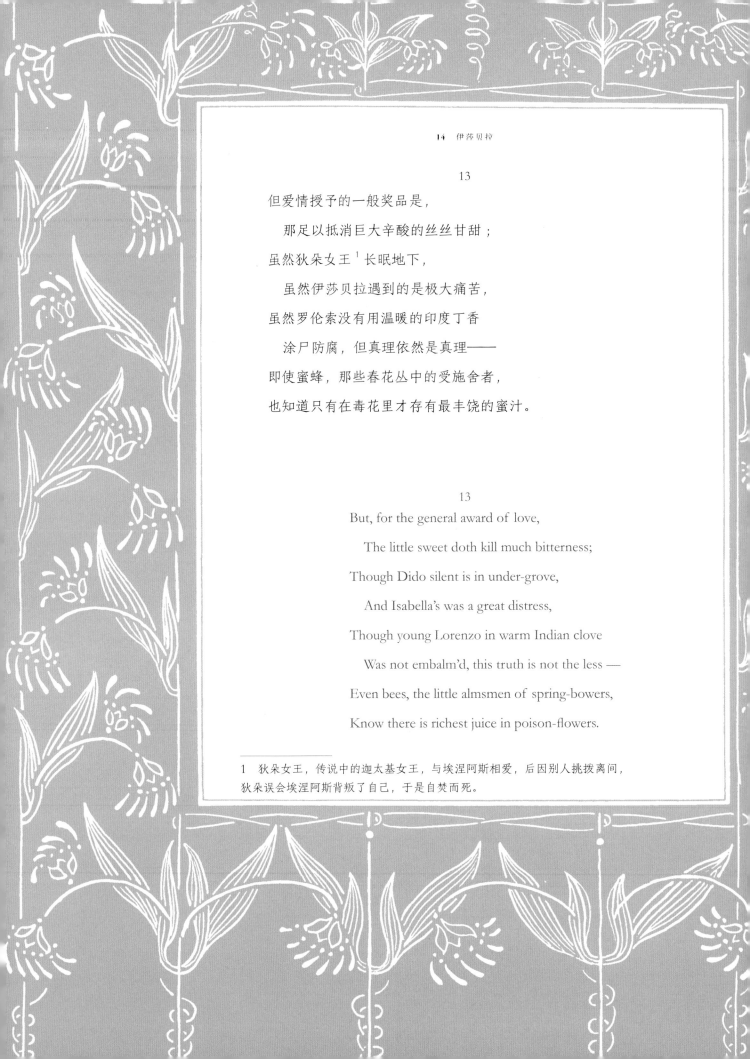

13

但爱情授予的一般奖品是，

　　那足以抵消巨大辛酸的丝丝甘甜；

虽然狄朵女王[1]长眠地下，

　　虽然伊莎贝拉遇到的是极大痛苦，

虽然罗伦索没有用温暖的印度丁香

　　涂尸防腐，但真理依然是真理——

即使蜜蜂，那些春花丛中的受施舍者，

也知道只有在毒花里才存有最丰饶的蜜汁。

13

But, for the general award of love,

　　The little sweet doth kill much bitterness;

Though Dido silent is in under-grove,

　　And Isabella's was a great distress,

Though young Lorenzo in warm Indian clove

　　Was not embalm'd, this truth is not the less —

Even bees, the little almsmen of spring-bowers,

Know there is richest juice in poison-flowers.

1　狄朵女王，传说中的迦太基女王，与埃涅阿斯相爱，后因别人挑拨离间，狄朵误会埃涅阿斯背叛了自己，于是自焚而死。

14

这位美丽女郎同两个哥哥居住，

　　因祖传的产业过得丰裕富足，

在火炬通明的矿山和嘈杂的工厂中，

　　许多双疲劳的手为他们而发肿，

许多曾一度强壮敏捷的身躯溶进

　　皮鞭打伤的血里；许多两眼

深陷的人整天站在炫目的河流里，

淘取漂流在水中的贵重金沙。

14

With her two brothers this fair lady dwelt,

　　Enriched from ancestral merchandize,

And for them many a weary hand did swelt

　　In torched mines and noisy factories,

And many once proud-quiver'd loins did melt

　　In blood from stinging whip; — with hollow eyes

Many all day in dazzling river stood,

To take the rich-ored driftings of the flood.

15

锡兰的潜水者[1]为他们屏住气息，

全身赤裸地走向饥饿的鲨鱼；

他的耳朵为他们涌出鲜血；海豹

为他们满身负箭，同可怜的小舟

僵死在寒冰上；单是为了他们，

成千上万的人在深重的苦难中煎熬，

他们一知半解地转动简易的轮盘，

为了挟住和剥皮，开动锋利的刑具。

15

For them the Ceylon diver held his breath,

And went all naked to the hungry shark;

For them his ears gush'd blood; for them in death

The seal on the cold ice with piteous bark

Lay full of darts; for them alone did seethe

A thousand men in troubles wide and dark:

Half-ignorant, they turn'd an easy wheel,

That set sharp racks at work, to pinch and peel.

---

1 指探寻珍珠的潜水者。

16

他们为什么自豪？因为他们的云石喷泉

　　比一个可怜人的泪泉涌得还急吗？

他们为什么自豪？因为他们的橘子山

　　爬起来比病院的扶梯还容易吗？

他们为什么自豪？因为他们注销的账册

　　比古希腊的歌曲还多吗？

他们为什么自豪？我们再高声地问：

凭荣耀之名起誓，他们为什么自豪？

16

Why were they proud? Because their marble founts

　　Gush'd with more pride than do a wretch's tears? —

Why were they proud? Because fair orange-mounts

　　Were of more soft ascent than lazar stairs? —

Why were they proud? Because red-lin'd accounts

　　Were richer than the songs of Grecian years? —

Why were they proud? again we ask aloud,

Why in the name of Glory were they proud?

17

可是这两个佛罗伦萨人在他们的

　　贪得无厌的骄傲和唯利是图的怯懦中

泰然自得，像两个隐藏在灵地上的

　　希伯来人，围着篱笆和葡萄园

不让乞丐窥探；如桅的森林中的鸷鹰——

　　追求钱财浮华而不倦的驮筐驴子——

抓取温和的离群者的敏捷的猫脚爪，——

西班牙、多斯加纳和马来西亚事务的通才。

17

Yet were these Florentines as self-retired

　　In hungry pride and gainful cowardice,

As two close Hebrews in that land inspired,

　　Paled in and vineyarded from beggar-spies;

The hawks of ship-mast forests — the untired

　　And pannier'd mules for ducats and old lies —

Quick cat's-paws on the generous stray-away, —

Great wits in Spanish, Tuscan, and Malay.

18

这两个管总账的人怎么能在

美丽的伊莎贝拉的温柔乡中监视她？

他们怎么能在罗伦索的眼睛里

发现一种不务正业的神色？

这在他们贪婪狡猾的眼中就是埃及的鼠疫！

这两个钱囊怎能分得清东和西？

可是他们这么做了——每个公平的商贾

都得留心身后，像被追逐的野兔那般。

18

How was it these same ledger-men could spy

Fair Isabella in her downy nest?

How could they find out in Lorenzo's eye

A straying from his toil? Hot Egypt's pest

Into their vision covetous and sly!

How could these money-bags see east and west? —

Yet so they did — and every dealer fair

Must see behind, as doth the hunted hare.

19

举世闻名的雄辩的卜伽丘啊！

　　我们如今应向你，向你那盛开的、

芬芳的桃金娘，向你那恋慕月亮的玫瑰，

　　向你那因再无法听到你的

古琵琶曲而变得更苍白的百合花，

　　恳求宽恕的恩典，因为我们冒昧地

写出与这样一个哀艳忧郁的

主题如此不相称的字句章节。

19

O eloquent and famed Boccaccio!

　　Of thee we now should ask forgiving boon,

And of thy spicy myrtles as they blow,

　　And of thy roses amorous of the moon,

And of thy lilies, that do paler grow

　　Now they can no more hear thy ghittern's tune,

For venturing syllables that ill beseem

The quiet glooms of such a piteous theme.

20

请你在这里赐予宽恕，然后这个故事

　　就将恰如其分地继续讲下去；

没有其他罪行或疯狂的攻击，

　　使由近代韵文写成的古代散文更美妙：

不论这诗章成功与否，它是为尊敬你，

　　和你那已逝的英灵而作；

它用英国语言的格律来代替你

在那北风号啸中的一个回声。

20

Grant thou a pardon here, and then the tale

　　Shall move on soberly, as it is meet;

There is no other crime, no mad assail

　　To make old prose in modern rhyme more sweet:

But it is done — succeed the verse or fail —

　　To honour thee, and thy gone spirit greet;

To stead thee as a verse in English tongue,

An echo of thee in the north-wind sung.

21

这两个兄弟凭许多迹象发现了

   罗伦索对他们的妹妹怀有的爱意，

她也深爱着他，各自直抒胸臆，

   吐露痛苦的相思，真是几近疯狂，

想到他，他们的贸易计划的佣仆，

   竟在他们妹妹的爱情中愉悦欢乐，

他们原来打算逐步以甘言诱引

她嫁给一个贵族及其橄榄树林。

21

These brethren having found by many signs

   What love Lorenzo for their sister had,

And how she lov'd him too, each unconfines

   His bitter thoughts to other, well nigh mad

That he, the servant of their trade designs,

   Should in their sister's love be blithe and glad,

When 'twas their plan to coax her by degrees

To some high noble and his olive-trees.

22

他们做了许多次充满妒意的商议，

　　他们多次独自咬紧自己的嘴唇，

才想出了一个万无一失的办法，

　　让那个年轻人赎清自己的罪行；

到最后，这两个本性残忍的人

　　用一柄锋利的刀把"仁慈"砍进了骨头；

因为他们决定在阴暗的森林里

把罗伦索杀死，并把他埋在那里。

22

And many a jealous conference had they,

　　And many times they bit their lips alone,

Before they fix'd upon a surest way

　　To make the youngster for his crime atone;

And at the last, these men of cruel clay

　　Cut Mercy with a sharp knife to the bone;

For they resolved in some forest dim

To kill Lorenzo, and there bury him.

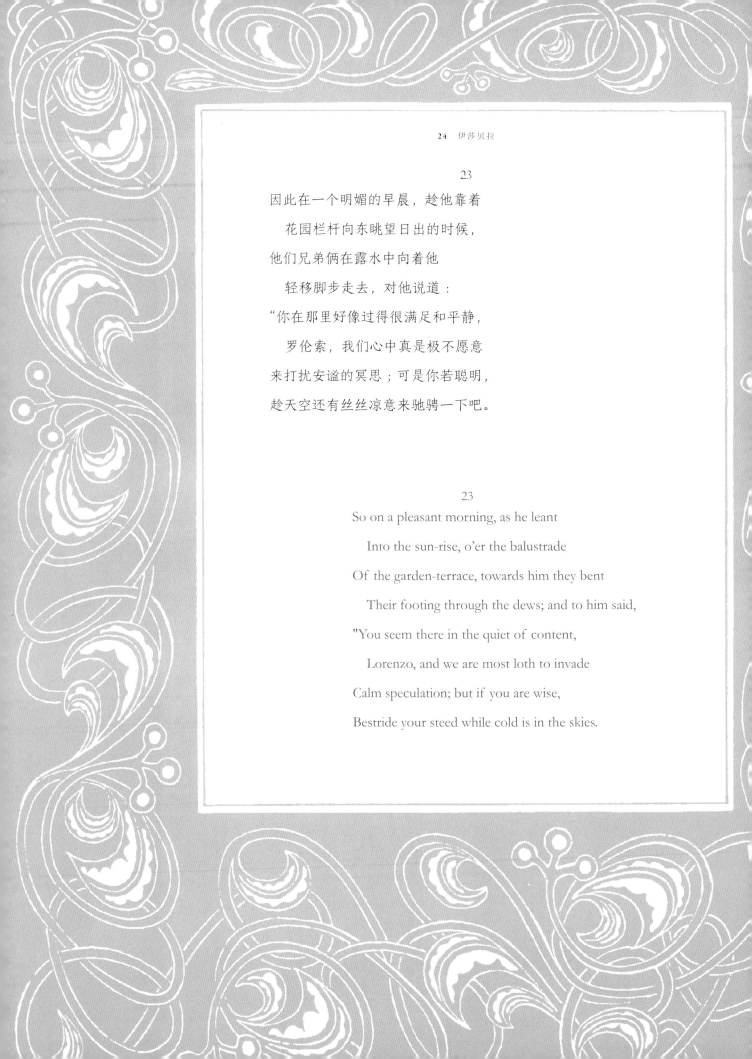

23

因此在一个明媚的早晨，趁他靠着

　　花园栏杆向东眺望日出的时候，

他们兄弟俩在露水中向着他

　　轻移脚步走去，对他说道：

"你在那里好像过得很满足和平静，

　　罗伦索，我们心中真是极不愿意

来打扰安谧的冥思；可是你若聪明，

趁天空还有丝丝凉意来驰骋一下吧。

23

So on a pleasant morning, as he leant

　　Into the sun-rise, o'er the balustrade

Of the garden-terrace, towards him they bent

　　Their footing through the dews; and to him said,

"You seem there in the quiet of content,

　　Lorenzo, and we are most loth to invade

Calm speculation; but if you are wise,

Bestride your steed while cold is in the skies.

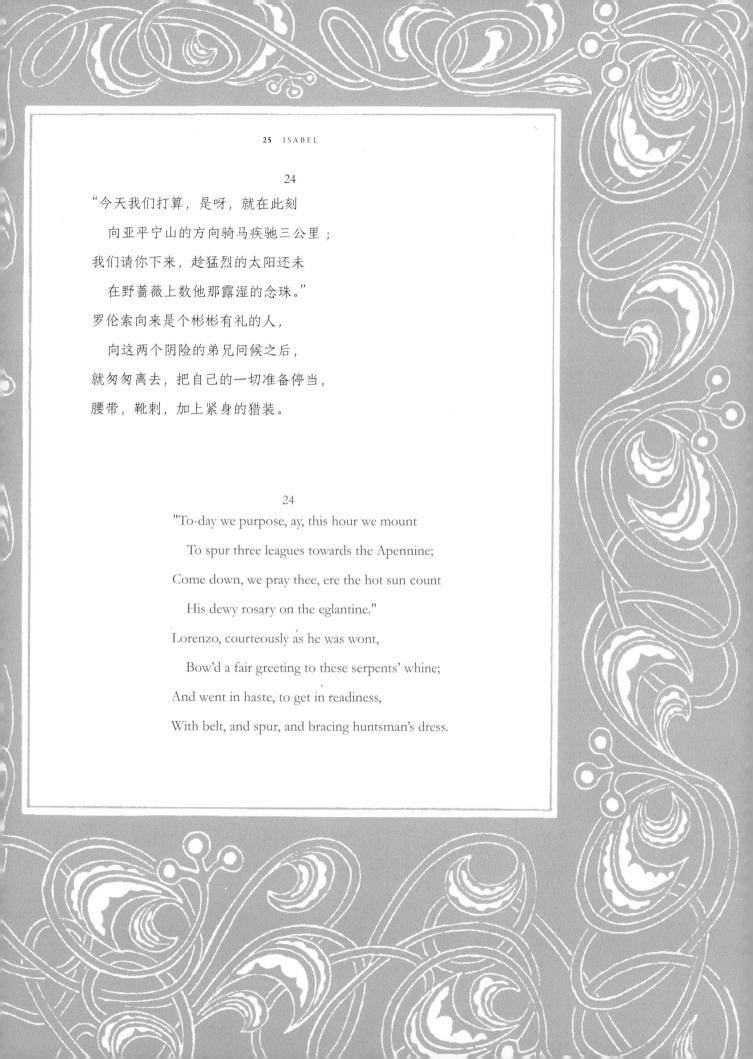

24

"今天我们打算，是呀，就在此刻

　　向亚平宁山的方向骑马疾驰三公里；

我们请你下来，趁猛烈的太阳还未

　　在野蔷薇上数他那露湿的念珠。"

罗伦索向来是个彬彬有礼的人，

　　向这两个阴险的弟兄问候之后，

就匆匆离去，把自己的一切准备停当，

腰带，靴刺，加上紧身的猎装。

24

"To-day we purpose, ay, this hour we mount

　　To spur three leagues towards the Apennine;

Come down, we pray thee, ere the hot sun count

　　His dewy rosary on the eglantine."

Lorenzo, courteously as he was wont,

　　Bow'd a fair greeting to these serpents' whine;

And went in haste, to get in readiness,

With belt, and spur, and bracing huntsman's dress.

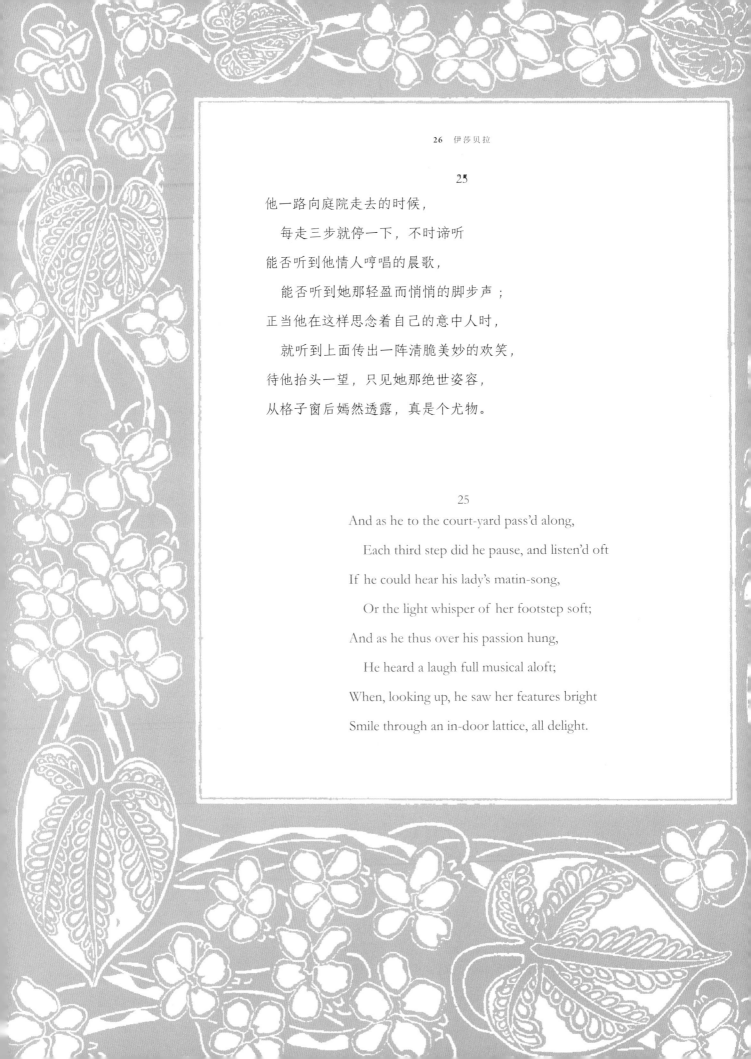

25

他一路向庭院走去的时候，

　　每走三步就停一下，不时谛听

能否听到他情人哼唱的晨歌，

　　能否听到她那轻盈而悄悄的脚步声；

正当他在这样思念着自己的意中人时，

　　就听到上面传出一阵清脆美妙的欢笑，

待他抬头一望，只见她那绝世姿容，

从格子窗后嫣然透露，真是个尤物。

25

And as he to the court-yard pass'd along,

　　Each third step did he pause, and listen'd oft

If he could hear his lady's matin-song,

　　Or the light whisper of her footstep soft;

And as he thus over his passion hung,

　　He heard a laugh full musical aloft;

When, looking up, he saw her features bright

Smile through an in-door lattice, all delight.

26

他说道："伊莎贝拉，我的爱人啊！

　　我因担心错过向你祝早安而痛苦。

唉！只是分别三个钟头我就这样急于

　　要压住种种忧虑，倘若失去了你

那又将怎样呢？但从多情的良宵中

　　我们必将获得白昼欠下的东西。

再会吧！我很快就会回来。"她应道：

"再会！"他离去时，她欢乐地歌唱。

26

"Love, Isabel!" said he, "I was in pain

　　Lest I should miss to bid thee a good morrow:

Ah! what if I should lose thee, when so fain

　　I am to stifle all the heavy sorrow

Of a poor three hours' absence? but we'll gain

　　Out of the amorous dark what day doth borrow.

Good bye! I'll soon be back." — "Good bye!" said she: —

And as he went she chanted merrily.

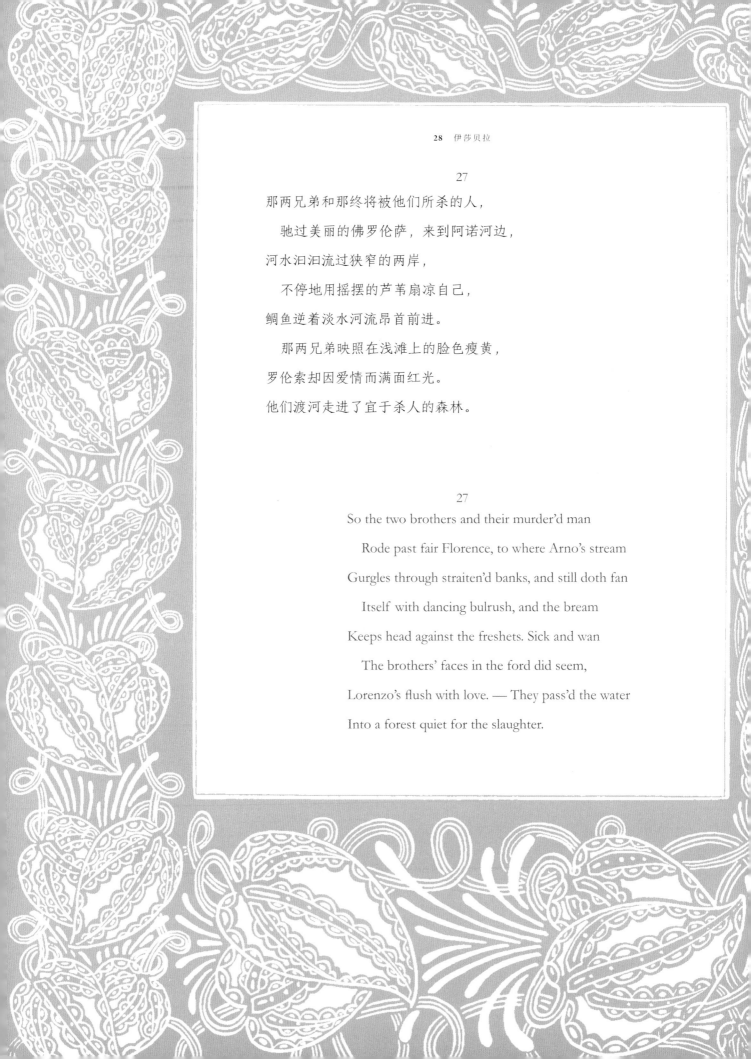

27

那两兄弟和那终将被他们所杀的人，

　　驰过美丽的佛罗伦萨，来到阿诺河边，

河水汩汩流过狭窄的两岸，

　　不停地用摇摆的芦苇扇凉自己，

鲷鱼逆着淡水河流昂首前进。

　　那两兄弟映照在浅滩上的脸色瘦黄，

罗伦索却因爱情而满面红光。

他们渡河走进了宜于杀人的森林。

27

So the two brothers and their murder'd man

　　Rode past fair Florence, to where Arno's stream

Gurgles through straiten'd banks, and still doth fan

　　Itself with dancing bulrush, and the bream

Keeps head against the freshets. Sick and wan

　　The brothers' faces in the ford did seem,

Lorenzo's flush with love. — They pass'd the water

Into a forest quiet for the slaughter.

28

罗伦索正是在那里被杀死并就地掩埋，

　　他那伟大的爱情也被埋葬在那树林中；

唉！一个灵魂这样获得解脱时，

　　只能在孤寂中悲痛——无法平静，

这种罪恶犹如从隐伏处窜出的猛犬；

　　他们把自己的剑在水中浸一下，

用痉挛似的刺马钉驱策马匹回家，

他们因成为杀人犯而显得更有身价。

28

There was Lorenzo slain and buried in,

　　There in that forest did his great love cease;

Ah! when a soul doth thus its freedom win,

　　It aches in loneliness — is ill at peace

As the break-covert blood-hounds of such sin:

　　They dipp'd their swords in the water, and did tease

Their horses homeward, with convulsed spur,

Each richer by his being a murderer.

29

他们告诉自己的妹妹，罗伦索如何

　　出于他们事务上极大的迫切

和需要——需要有个可靠的人手，

　　就急匆匆地乘船去了外国。

可怜的女郎呀！穿上你那窒闷的丧服，

　　立即逃出"希望"那可恶的手掌吧！

今天你不会看到他，明天也不会，

之后的每一天都将是充满悲痛的日子。

29

They told their sister how, with sudden speed,

　　Lorenzo had ta'en ship for foreign lands,

Because of some great urgency and need

　　In their affairs, requiring trusty hands.

Poor Girl! put on thy stifling widow's weed,

　　And 'scape at once from Hope's accursed bands;

To-day thou wilt not see him, nor to-morrow,

And the next day will be a day of sorrow.

30

她为将再也无法得到欢乐而独自流泪，

　　她从早悲伤地哭泣到夜色降临。

以后，不能再相亲相爱，多悲惨啊！

　　她独自恍然凝思过去的欢乐，

仿佛在暮色苍茫中看到他的身影，

　　不禁向四周的沉寂轻轻地呻吟，

将自己白璧无瑕的双臂对空张开，

又横在睡榻上低声呢喃："在哪儿呀在哪儿？"

30

She weeps alone for pleasures not to be;

　　Sorely she wept until the night came on,

And then, instead of love, O misery!

　　She brooded o'er the luxury alone:

His image in the dusk she seem'd to see,

　　And to the silence made a gentle moan,

Spreading her perfect arms upon the air,

And on her couch low murmuring "Where? O where?"

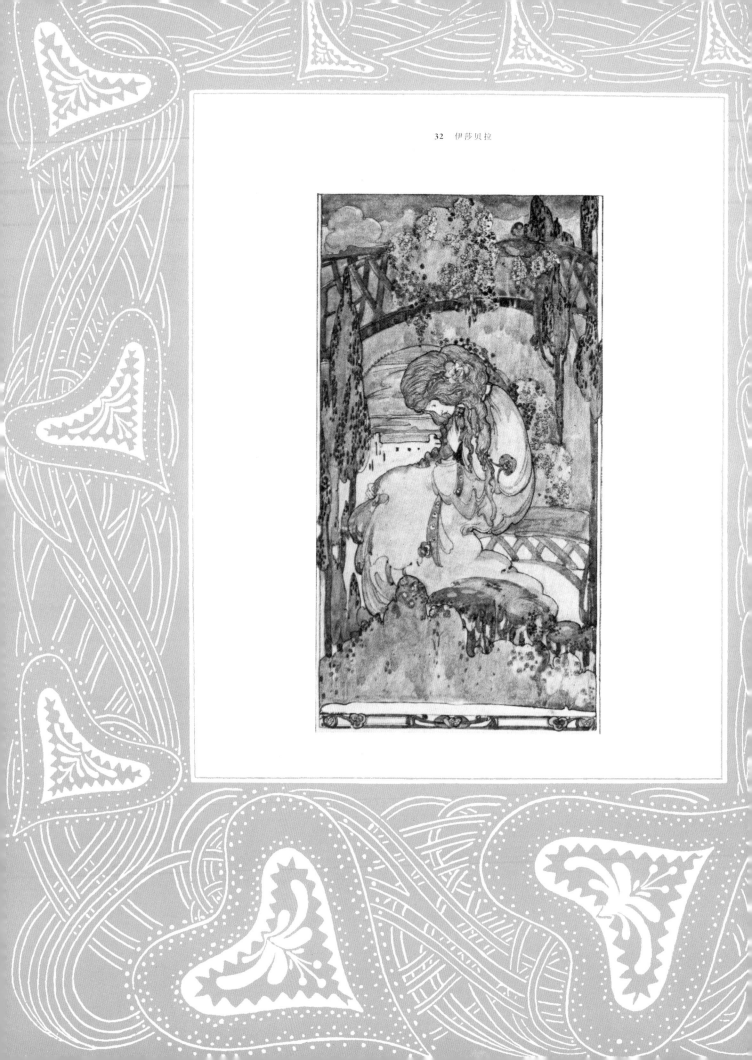

31

但"爱情"的表妹"自私自利"并没有长久

　　而强烈地驻守在那孤单的胸腔里；

她为那千金一刻的良宵而感到迫切的渴望，

　　以患了热病似的不安等待着那时光——

这样并不长久；因为不久以后

　　一些更高的念头，一些更强烈的兴味，

悲惨地占据了她的心，抑制不住的激情，

和她对那辛苦跋涉的途中情人的忧思。

31

But Selfishness, Love's cousin, held not long

　　Its fiery vigil in her single breast;

She fretted for the golden hour, and hung

　　Upon the time with feverish unrest —

Not long — for soon into her heart a throng

　　Of higher occupants, a richer zest,

Came tragic; passion not to be subdued,

And sorrow for her love in travels rude.

32

在仲秋时节，一到了傍晚，

　　冬天的气息便从远方吹来，

病恹恹的西风不断地夺去

　　一些黄金色彩，在灌木丛

和树叶中间奏一支死之圆舞曲，

　　等一切都变得光秃秃，才敢走出

北方的洞窟。可爱的伊莎贝拉

也因逐渐衰颓而变得丑陋。

32

In the mid days of autumn, on their eves

　　The breath of Winter comes from far away,

And the sick west continually bereaves

　　Of some gold tinge, and plays a roundelay

Of death among the bushes and the leaves,

　　To make all bare before he dares to stray

From his north cavern. So sweet Isabel

By gradual decay from beauty fell,

33

因为罗伦索不回来。她时常

　　眼睛黯淡无光竭力保持镇定，

问她两个哥哥，究竟是什么牢狱似的国家

　　能使他离开得那么久？他们一次又一次地

撒个谎来使她安静。他们的罪恶

　　罩住他们，像从欣嫩谷生出的一缕烟；

他们每天晚上在梦中高声呻吟，

看到妹妹穿着雪白的尸衾。

33

Because Lorenzo came not. Oftentimes

　　She ask'd her brothers, with an eye all pale,

Striving to be itself, what dungeon climes

　　Could keep him off so long? They spake a tale

Time after time, to quiet her. Their crimes

　　Came on them, like a smoke from Hinnom's vale;

And every night in dreams they groan'd aloud,

To see their sister in her snowy shroud.

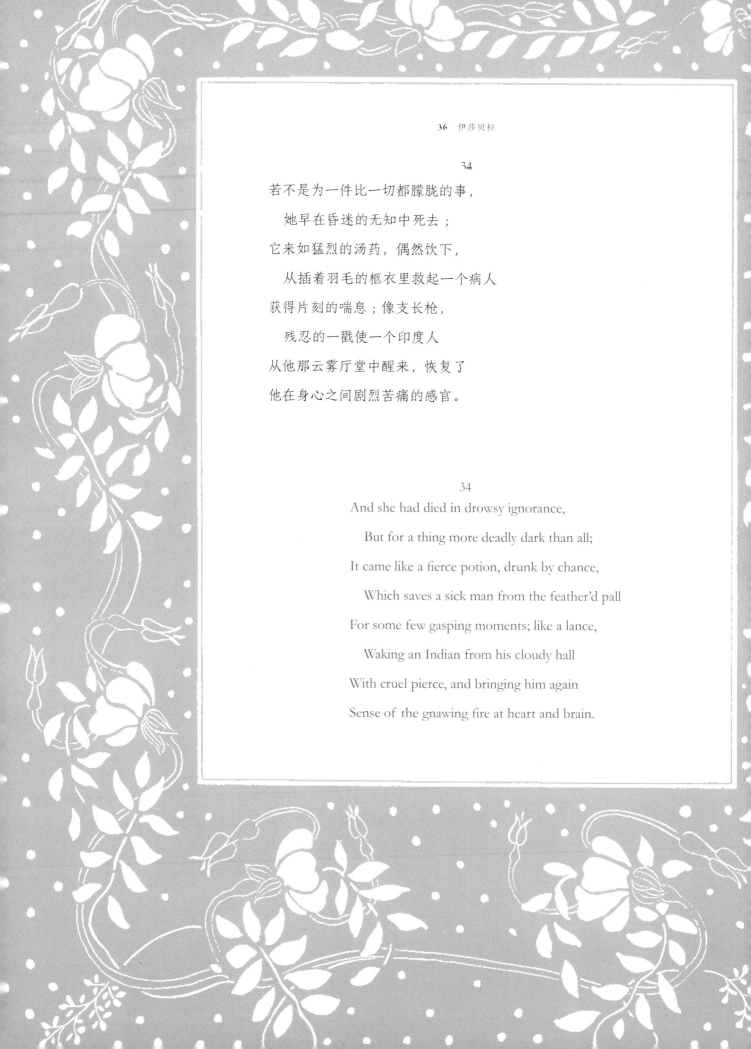

34

若不是为一件比一切都朦胧的事，

　　她早在昏迷的无知中死去；

它来如猛烈的汤药，偶然饮下，

　　从插着羽毛的柩衣里救起一个病人

获得片刻的喘息；像支长枪，

　　残忍的一戳使一个印度人

从他那云雾厅堂中醒来，恢复了

他在身心之间剧烈苦痛的感官。

34

And she had died in drowsy ignorance,

　　But for a thing more deadly dark than all;

It came like a fierce potion, drunk by chance,

　　Which saves a sick man from the feather'd pall

For some few gasping moments; like a lance,

　　Waking an Indian from his cloudy hall

With cruel pierce, and bringing him again

Sense of the gnawing fire at heart and brain.

35

那是一个梦。在昏睡的阴暗中，

　　正是沉闷的午夜时分，罗伦索

站在她床榻边流泪：森林的坟墓

　　损毁了他光泽的头发，在生前

那头发的光芒可以射向太阳，如今他的嘴唇

　　已变得冰冷，他那害相思的声音

不再像琵琶声般动听，他那塞满泥的耳朵

被他的泪水划出了一道泥泞的槽沟。

35

It was a vision. — In the drowsy gloom,

　　The dull of midnight, at her couch's foot

Lorenzo stood, and wept: the forest tomb

　　Had marr'd his glossy hair which once could shoot

Lustre into the sun, and put cold doom

　　Upon his lips, and taken the soft lute

From his lorn voice, and past his loamed ears

Had made a miry channel for his tears.

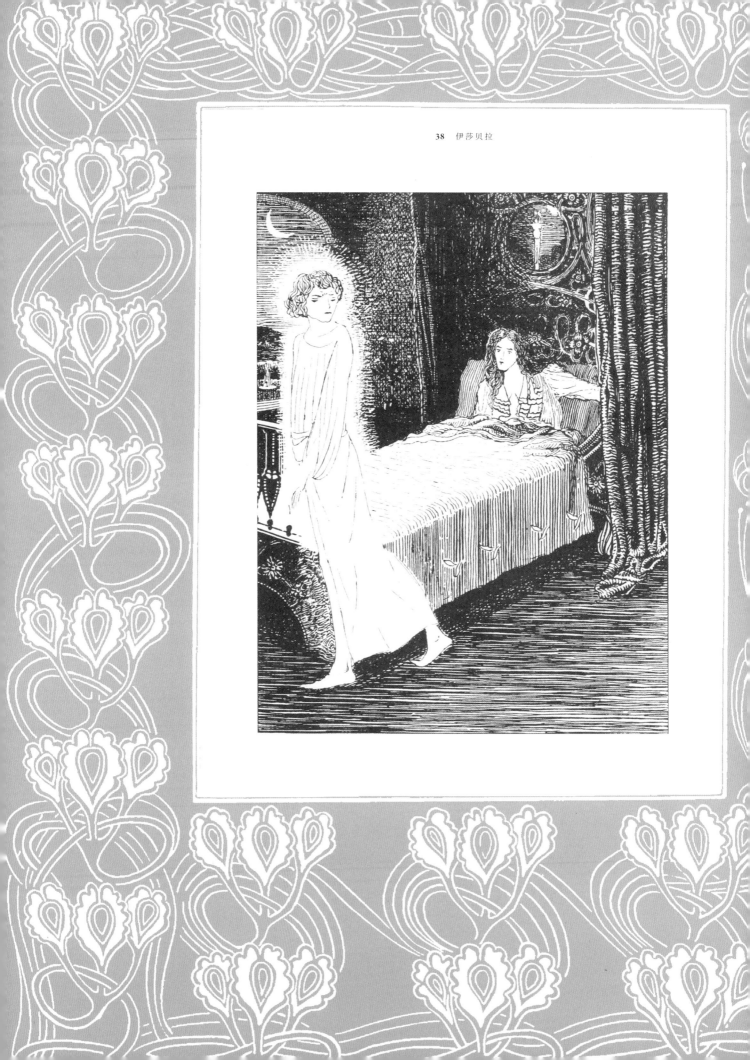

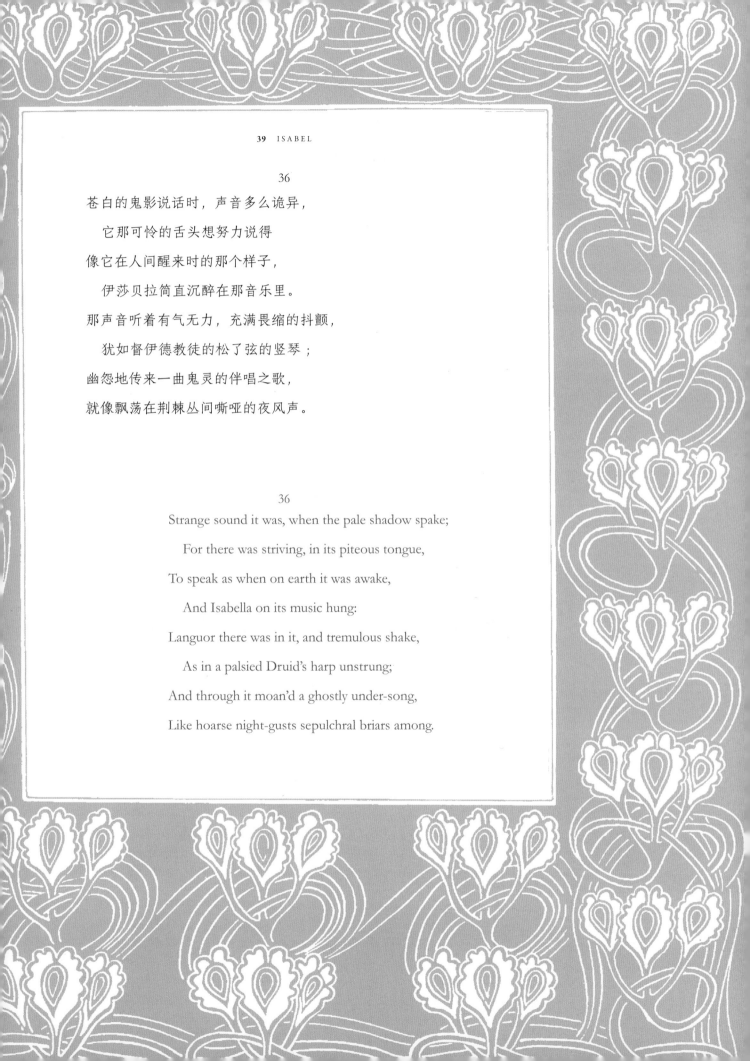

36

苍白的鬼影说话时，声音多么诡异，

　　它那可怜的舌头想努力说得

像它在人间醒来时的那个样子，

　　伊莎贝拉简直沉醉在那音乐里。

那声音听着有气无力，充满畏缩的抖颤，

　　犹如督伊德教徒的松了弦的竖琴；

幽怨地传来一曲鬼灵的伴唱之歌，

就像飘荡在荆棘丛间嘶哑的夜风声。

36

Strange sound it was, when the pale shadow spake;

　　For there was striving, in its piteous tongue,

To speak as when on earth it was awake,

　　And Isabella on its music hung:

Languor there was in it, and tremulous shake,

　　As in a palsied Druid's harp unstrung;

And through it moan'd a ghostly under-song,

Like hoarse night-gusts sepulchral briars among.

37

那鬼灵的眼睛虽然疯狂，却依然

　　因爱情而闪着露珠般的光芒，这光的魔力

使这可怜的姑娘免却一切虚惊，

　　同时它把深夜阴森时光的

可怖之织物一一拆开——骄傲和贪婪的

　　谋害的毒心——那森林里的

黑暗如盖的松木——和那草泥地的山谷，

他就在那里被刺倒下，默默无言。

37

Its eyes, though wild, were still all dewy bright

　　With love, and kept all phantom fear aloof

From the poor girl by magic of their light,

　　The while it did unthread the horrid woof

Of the late darken'd time, — the murderous spite

　　Of pride and avarice, — the dark pine roof

In the forest, — and the sodden turfed dell,

Where, without any word, from stabs he fell.

38

它还说道："伊莎贝拉，我的爱人呀！

　　红色的越橘树在我头顶低垂，

一块巨大的燧石压住我的双脚；

　　山毛榉和高大的栗树在我四周撒下

叶子和刺人的坚果；那河对面

　　羊栏内的一阵鸣叫传到我的墓床；

去吧，在我的石楠花上洒阵泪水，

泪水必将安慰坟墓内的我。

38

Saying moreover, "Isabel, my sweet!

　　Red whortle-berries droop above my head,

And a large flint-stone weighs upon my feet;

　　Around me beeches and high chestnuts shed

Their leaves and prickly nuts; a sheep-fold bleat

　　Comes from beyond the river to my bed:

Go, shed one tear upon my heather-bloom,

And it shall comfort me within the tomb.

39

"我如今是个阴魂了，唉！唉！

　　在人类天性的边缘上孤孤单单

居住着：我独自吟唱神圣的弥撒，

　　生命的细小声音在我周围鸣响，

正午时分光洁的蜜蜂飞过田野，

　　好多礼拜堂的钟声在报时辰，

使我彻骨痛苦：这些声音对我变得

陌生了，而你是在遥远遥远的人间。

39

"I am a shadow now, alas! alas!

　　Upon the skirts of human-nature dwelling

Alone: I chant alone the holy mass,

　　While little sounds of life are round me knelling,

And glossy bees at noon do fieldward pass,

　　And many a chapel bell the hour is telling,

Paining me through: those sounds grow strange to me,

And thou art distant in Humanity.

40

"我知道过去的事，我完全感觉得到现在的事，

　　假使阴灵能够发狂，我会暴跳如雷；

虽然我忘却了人间幸福的滋味，

　　但那种苍白使我的坟墓温暖，

仿佛我从光辉的深渊中挑了个天使

　　做我的配偶：你的苍白使我喜欢；

你的美丽渐渐被我爱好起来，我觉得

一种更伟大的爱暗暗流彻我的骨髓。"

40

"I know what was, I feel full well what is,

　　And I should rage, if spirits could go mad;

Though I forget the taste of earthly bliss,

　　That paleness warms my grave, as though I had

A Seraph chosen from the bright abyss

　　To be my spouse: thy paleness makes me glad;

Thy beauty grows upon me, and I feel

A greater love through all my essence steal."

41

那阴灵哀伤地道了声"珍重！"——就此消失，

　　把那浑噩的黑暗留在缓慢的骚扰中；

如同子夜时分的睡眠被剥夺，

　　只因想着坎坷的时光与无益的辛勤，

我们把自己的眼睛埋在枕头深处，

　　看到金片般的阴暗翻腾滚沸：

那鬼灵使伊莎贝拉的眼皮作痛，

黎明时分她猛然张开惺忪眼睛。

41

The Spirit mourn'd "Adieu!" — dissolv'd, and left

　　The atom darkness in a slow turmoil;

As when of healthful midnight sleep bereft,

　　Thinking on rugged hours and fruitless toil,

We put our eyes into a pillowy cleft,

　　And see the spangly gloom froth up and boil:

It made sad Isabella's eyelids ache,

And in the dawn she started up awake;

42

"哈！哈！"她说道，"我不知这艰苦的人生，

　　我原以为最坏的是简单的悲惨；

我原以为是某个命运之神派给我们

　　欢乐或斗争——幸福的日子或死亡；

哪知还有犯罪——一把兄弟的血腥的刀！

　　可爱的阴魂呀，你开导了我的无知：

我要为此访谒你，亲吻你的眼睛，

朝朝暮暮在诸天之中向你问候。"

42

"Ha! ha!" said she, "I knew not this hard life,

　　I thought the worst was simple misery;

I thought some Fate with pleasure or with strife

　　Portion'd us — happy days, or else to die;

But there is crime — a brother's bloody knife!

　　Sweet Spirit, thou hast school'd my infancy:

I'll visit thee for this, and kiss thine eyes,

And greet thee morn and even in the skies."

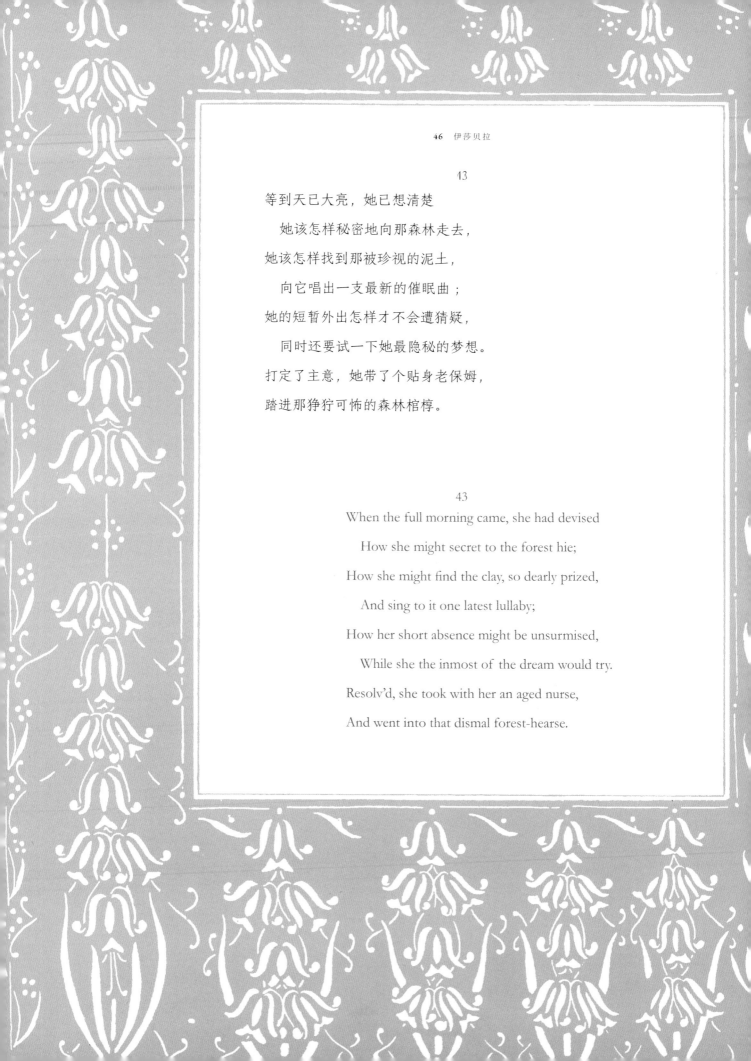

13

等到天已大亮，她已想清楚

　　她该怎样秘密地向那森林走去，

她该怎样找到那被珍视的泥土，

　　向它唱出一支最新的催眠曲；

她的短暂外出怎样才不会遭猜疑，

　　同时还要试一下她最隐秘的梦想。

打定了主意，她带了个贴身老保姆，

踏进那狰狞可怖的森林棺椁。

43

When the full morning came, she had devised

　　How she might secret to the forest hie;

How she might find the clay, so dearly prized,

　　And sing to it one latest lullaby;

How her short absence might be unsurmised,

　　While she the inmost of the dream would try.

Resolv'd, she took with her an aged nurse,

And went into that dismal forest-hearse.

44

看呀，她们沿着河边蹑足前行时，

　　她如何向那年老的妇人低声说话，

把那广阔的平地观望了一遍之后，

　　拿出一把刀给老妇人看。——"孩子呀，

什么热病似的烈火在你心内燃烧？——

　　遇到什么称心事你才能再含笑呢？"——

到黄昏时，她们找到了罗伦索的泥圹；

那燧石在那儿，浆果在他的头旁。

44

See, as they creep along the river side,

　　How she doth whisper to that aged Dame,

And, after looking round the champaign wide,

　　Shows her a knife. — "What feverous hectic flame

Burns in thee, child? — What good can thee betide,

　　That thou should'st smile again?" — The evening came,

And they had found Lorenzo's earthy bed;

The flint was there, the berries at his head.

45

谁不曾在绿色的墓园中闲逛，

　　让自己的精神，像只鬼灵的田鼠，

钻过黏泞的泥土和坚硬的卵石，

　　看脑壳、棺中的白骨和尸衣；

怜悯饥饿的死神所损毁的每种形体，

　　而再一次以人类的灵魂来填充它？

这就是伊莎贝拉跪在罗伦索旁边时

所感觉到的，好像在过节日啊！

45

Who hath not loiter'd in a green church-yard,

　　And let his spirit, like a demon-mole,

Work through the clayey soil and gravel hard,

　　To see scull, coffin'd bones, and funeral stole;

Pitying each form that hungry Death hath marr'd,

　　And filling it once more with human soul?

Ah! this is holiday to what was felt

When Isabella by Lorenzo knelt.

46

她瞪眼凝视那刚盖上的泥土，

　　仿佛一眼就看穿了全部秘密；

她清清楚楚地看出，正如别人的眼睛

　　会认出清泉底部的苍白的肢体；

她似乎在那杀人的地点上生了根，

　　如同山谷里的一枝土生的百合花；

继而她突然间抽出刀来开始挖掘，

比掘金宝的守财奴还要狂热。

46

She gaz'd into the fresh-thrown mould, as though

　　One glance did fully all its secrets tell;

Clearly she saw, as other eyes would know

　　Pale limbs at bottom of a crystal well;

Upon the murderous spot she seem'd to grow,

　　Like to a native lily of the dell:

Then with her knife, all sudden, she began

To dig more fervently than misers can.

47

她不久就掘出了一只泥污的手套，

　　她曾在那上面用丝线绣过紫红花样；

她用比石头更冷的嘴唇亲吻它，

　　把它放在怀中，它在那里

变得干燥了，并且把那些造来

　　使婴孩不啼不哭的妙物[1]完全冻结；

于是她又开始挖掘；她的忧虑并不停止，

时常把垂挂的长发抹向身后。

47

Soon she turn'd up a soiled glove, whereon

　　Her silk had play'd in purple phantasies,

She kiss'd it with a lip more chill than stone,

　　And put it in her bosom, where it dries

And freezes utterly unto the bone

　　Those dainties made to still an infant's cries:

Then 'gan she work again; nor stay'd her care,

But to throw back at times her veiling hair.

1　指母亲的乳房。

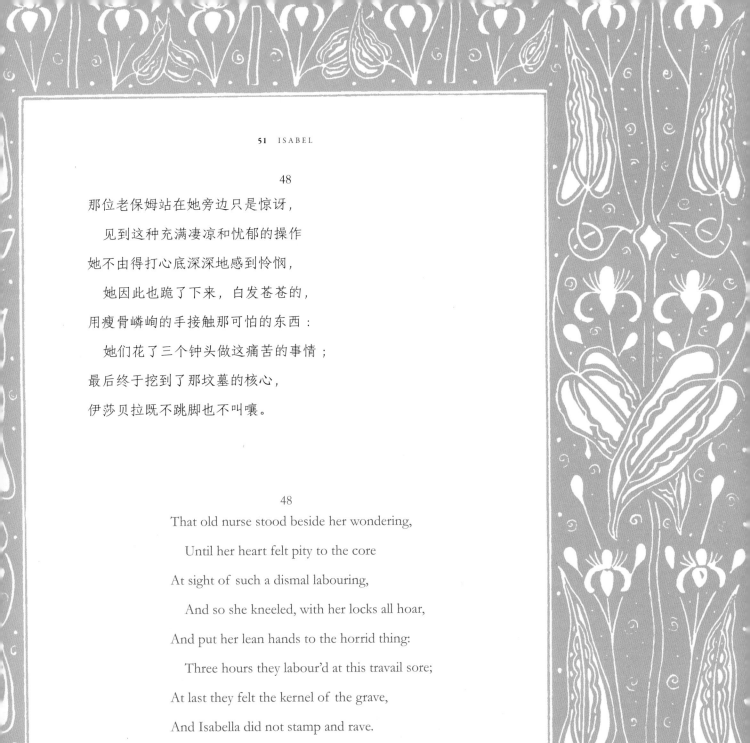

48

那位老保姆站在她旁边只是惊讶，

　　见到这种充满凄凉和忧郁的操作

她不由得打心底深深地感到怜悯，

　　她因此也跪了下来，白发苍苍的，

用瘦骨嶙峋的手接触那可怕的东西：

　　她们花了三个钟头做这痛苦的事情；

最后终于挖到了那坟墓的核心，

伊莎贝拉既不跳脚也不叫嚷。

48

That old nurse stood beside her wondering,

　　Until her heart felt pity to the core

At sight of such a dismal labouring,

　　And so she kneeled, with her locks all hoar,

And put her lean hands to the horrid thing:

　　Three hours they labour'd at this travail sore;

At last they felt the kernel of the grave,

And Isabella did not stamp and rave.

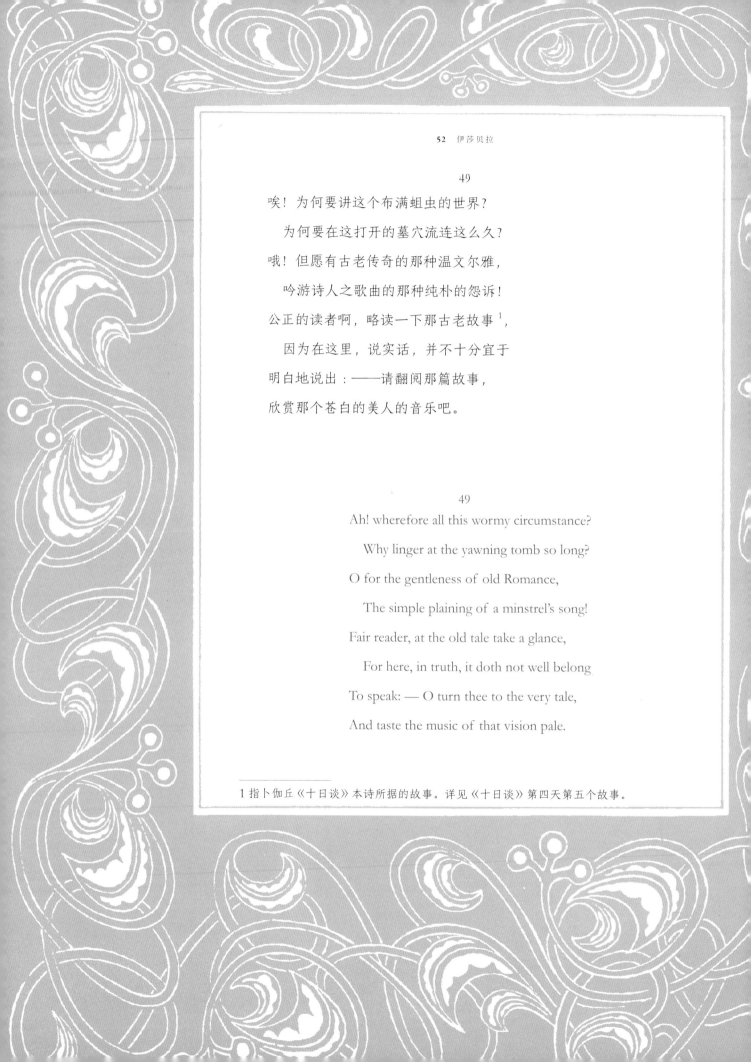

49

唉！为何要讲这个布满蛆虫的世界？

　为何要在这打开的墓穴流连这么久？

哦！但愿有古老传奇的那种温文尔雅，

　吟游诗人之歌曲的那种纯朴的怨诉！

公正的读者啊，略读一下那古老故事[1]，

　因为在这里，说实话，并不十分宜于

明白地说出：——请翻阅那篇故事，

欣赏那个苍白的美人的音乐吧。

49

Ah! wherefore all this wormy circumstance?

　Why linger at the yawning tomb so long?

O for the gentleness of old Romance,

　The simple plaining of a minstrel's song!

Fair reader, at the old tale take a glance,

　For here, in truth, it doth not well belong

To speak: — O turn thee to the very tale,

And taste the music of that vision pale.

1 指卜伽丘《十日谈》本诗所据的故事。详见《十日谈》第四天第五个故事。

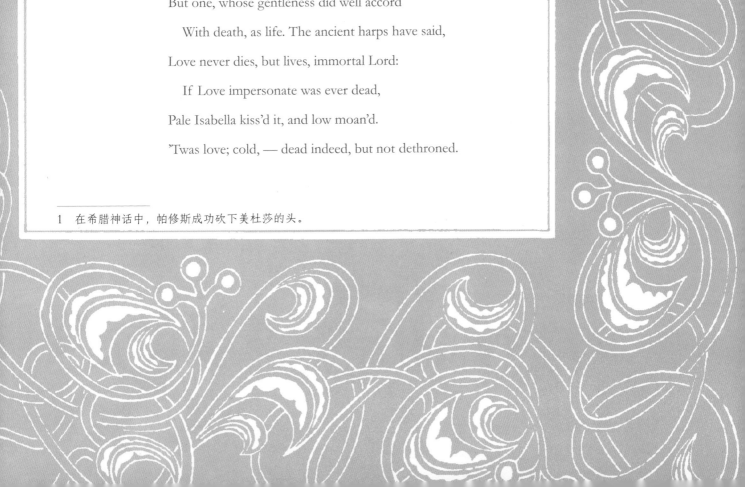

50

她们用比帕修斯[1]的宝剑略钝的钢刀

　　砍掉了一个并非无形的怪物的头，

然而这样一个人的头，他的温存

　　完全与死相称，犹如与生相称一般。

古琴曲上说过，爱决不会死，而会永生，

　　不朽的主啊：如果爱的化身曾经死过，

苍白的伊莎贝拉曾同它接吻，低声悲叹。

这就是爱；冰凉——的确死了，但未被废黜。

50

With duller steel than the Perséan sword

　　They cut away no formless monster's head,

But one, whose gentleness did well accord

　　With death, as life. The ancient harps have said,

Love never dies, but lives, immortal Lord:

　　If Love impersonate was ever dead,

Pale Isabella kiss'd it, and low moan'd.

'Twas love; cold, — dead indeed, but not dethroned.

1　在希腊神话中，帕修斯成功砍下美杜莎的头。

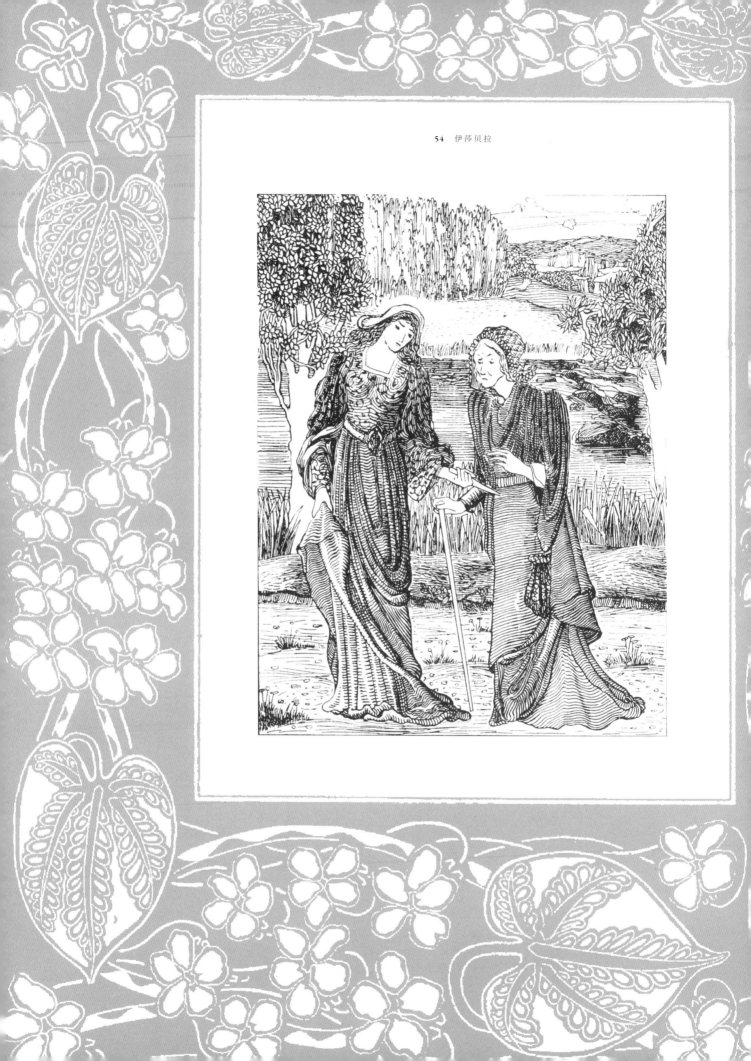

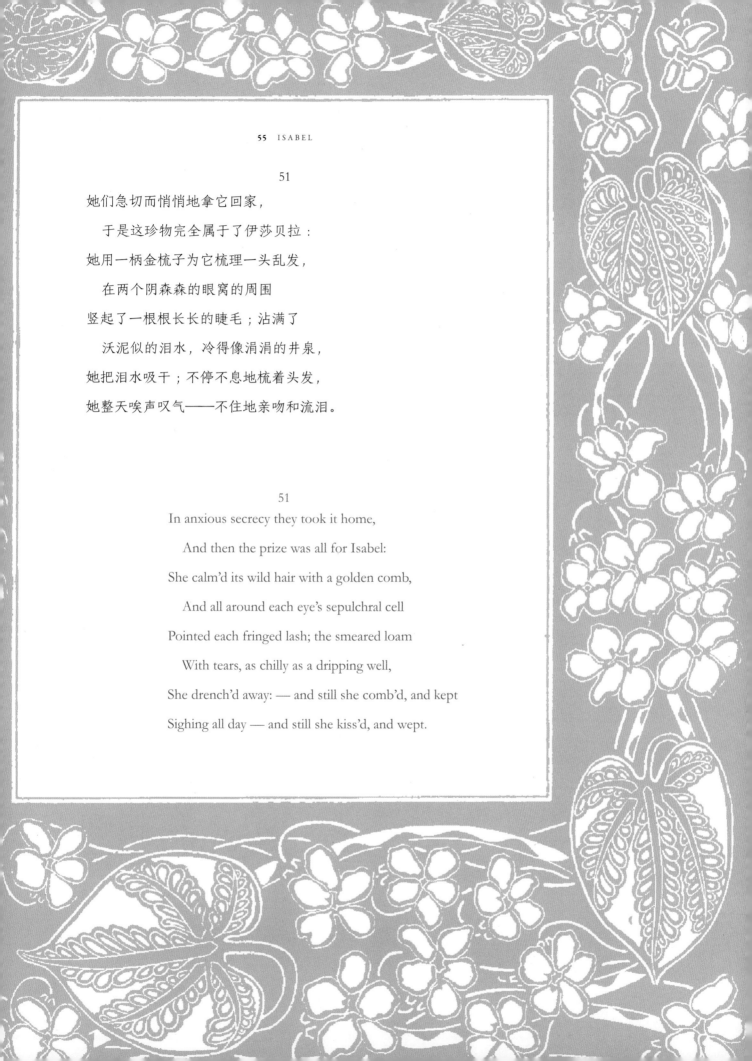

51

她们急切而悄悄地拿它回家，

　　于是这珍物完全属于了伊莎贝拉：

她用一柄金梳子为它梳理一头乱发，

　　在两个阴森森的眼窝的周围

竖起了一根根长长的睫毛；沾满了

　　沃泥似的泪水，冷得像涓涓的井泉，

她把泪水吸干；不停不息地梳着头发，

她整天唉声叹气——不住地亲吻和流泪。

51

In anxious secrecy they took it home,

　　And then the prize was all for Isabel:

She calm'd its wild hair with a golden comb,

　　And all around each eye's sepulchral cell

Pointed each fringed lash; the smeared loam

　　With tears, as chilly as a dripping well,

She drench'd away: — and still she comb'd, and kept

Sighing all day — and still she kiss'd, and wept.

52

她把头颅裹进一条丝巾里，——

　　用从阿拉伯折来的珍贵的花朵，

蛇形喇叭里芳芬地渗流出来的

　　沁人心脾的鲜浆，让这条丝巾

香气扑鼻；她选了园中一只花盆

　　给那头颅作坟墓，把它放在里面，

用泥土掩盖起来，在上面栽植

美丽的罗勒花，用泪水使它始终潮湿。

52

Then in a silken scarf, — sweet with the dews

　　Of precious flowers pluck'd in Araby,

And divine liquids come with odorous ooze

　　Through the cold serpent-pipe refreshfully, —

She wrapp'd it up; and for its tomb did choose

　　A garden-pot, wherein she laid it by,

And cover'd it with mould, and o'er it set

Sweet basil, which her tears kept ever wet.

53

她忘记了星辰、月亮和太阳，

　　忘记了树木之上的蓝色天空，

忘记了清水奔流其间的溪谷，

　　忘记了清冷秋日里刮起的风；

也不清楚白昼在何时消尽，

　　新的一天如何开始；只是恬静地

始终低头守着她那美丽的罗勒花，

用自己的泪水使它永远湿润。

53

And she forgot the stars, the moon, and sun,

　　And she forgot the blue above the trees,

And she forgot the dells where waters run,

　　And she forgot the chilly autumn breeze;

She had no knowledge when the day was done,

　　And the new morn she saw not: but in peace

Hung over her sweet basil evermore,

And moisten'd it with tears unto the core.

54

她就这么用稀薄的眼泪喂养着它，

    因此它长得又密，又绿，又美，

闻起来比佛罗伦萨城中

    任何一盆同类的罗勒花更为芬芳；

因为它还从人类的恐惧，

    从那密封不露的速朽的头颅里吸取

养分和活力：因此那被珍藏的珠宝

显露了出来，展开馨香的嫩叶。

54

And so she ever fed it with thin tears,

    Whence thick, and green, and beautiful it grew,

So that it smelt more balmy than its peers

    Of basil-tufts in Florence; for it drew

Nurture besides, and life, from human fears,

    From the fast mouldering head there shut from view:

So that the jewel, safely casketed,

Came forth, and in perfumed leafits spread.

55

"悲哀"呀，在这里停留一会儿吧！

　"音乐"呀"音乐"，沮丧地吹奏吧！

"回声"呀"回声"，从一些阴沉、无名、

　被遗忘的岛屿上向我们发出悲叹吧！

忧愁的众魂，抬起你们的头微笑吧，

　可爱的众魂啊，沉重地抬起你们的头，

在柏树枝杈间的幽暗中透下一片青光，

用银色的苍白浅染你们的云石墓吧。

55

O Melancholy, linger here awhile!

　O Music, Music, breathe despondingly!

O Echo, Echo, from some sombre isle,

　Unknown, Lethean, sigh to us — O sigh!

Spirits in grief, lift up your heads, and smile;

　Lift up your heads, sweet Spirits, heavily,

And make a pale light in your cypress glooms,

Tinting with silver wan your marble tombs.

56

你们所有的悲痛之音啊，从悲切的

　　墨尔波墨涅[1]的深喉中向这里哀号吧！

按照悲惨的序列拨动青铜的七弦琴，

　　把弦线拨动成一支神秘之曲；

逆风发出悲恸和颓丧的声音吧；

　　因为单纯质朴的伊莎贝拉不久

就将被列入亡魂的名册之中：她日趋枯萎，

有如印第安人为取香汁而割开的棕榈。

56

Moan hither, all ye syllables of woe,

　　From the deep throat of sad Melpomene!

Through bronzed lyre in tragic order go,

　　And touch the strings into a mystery;

Sound mournfully upon the winds and low;

　　For simple Isabel is soon to be

Among the dead: She withers, like a palm

Cut by an Indian for its juicy balm.

---

1 希腊神话中的哀曲女神，文艺九女神之一。

57

但愿能听任这株棕榈自行枯萎；

　　也不要让寒冬使它在临终时分战栗！——

不可能如此——那两个阿堵物[1]的崇拜者，

　　她那两个哥哥，已经注意到泪水不断地

从她失神的眼中涌出；她亲族中

　　的许多好奇者也无不感到惊奇：

一个注定要做贵族的新娘

竟将青春、美貌和嫁妆全都抛在一旁。

57

O leave the palm to wither by itself;

　　Let not quick Winter chill its dying hour! —

It may not be — those Baälites of pelf,

　　Her brethren, noted the continual shower

From her dead eyes; and many a curious elf,

　　Among her kindred, wonder'd that such dower

Of youth and beauty should be thrown aside

By one mark'd out to be a noble's bride.

1　在《世说新语》中，"阿堵物"是对钱的蔑称。原文此处对应的词为"pelf"，意"不义之财"。此处保留了译者最初的译法。

58

而让她那两个哥哥尤为好奇的是，

　　她为什么要坐在罗勒花旁垂头丧气，

而罗勒花为什么能长得如此茂盛，好像着了魔力；

　　他们更好奇这件事有什么意义：

他们当然无法相信，像这样

　　一种简直是虚无的东西竟有力量，

使她弃绝自己美妙的青春，人间的欢乐，

甚至对自己迟迟不归的情人的思念。

58

And, furthermore, her brethren wonder'd much

　　Why she sat drooping by the basil green,

And why it flourish'd, as by magic touch;

　　Greatly they wonder'd what the thing might mean:

They could not surely give belief, that such

　　A very nothing would have power to wean

Her from her own fair youth, and pleasures gay,

And even remembrance of her love's delay.

59

因此他们守候着一个能探出

　　这个隐秘怪念的时机；但守候多久

都是枉然；因为她难得去教堂忏悔，

　　也难得感到任何饥饿的痛苦。

她出家门，就匆匆归来，快得

　　像鸟儿振翼再飞回来伏窝；

然后像母鸡般耐心，坐在那里

守着她的罗勒花，在长发后流泪。

59

Therefore they watch'd a time when they might sift

　　This hidden whim; and long they watch'd in vain;

For seldom did she go to chapel-shrift,

　　And seldom felt she any hunger-pain;

And when she left, she hurried back, as swift

　　As bird on wing to breast its eggs again;

And, patient as a hen-bird, sat her there

Beside her basil, weeping through her hair.

60

他们还是想办法偷走了那罗勒花盆，

　　拿到隐秘的地方细细查看：

那东西虽被绿色和青黑色的斑点

　　毁坏，却被他们认出是罗伦索的脸；

他们已经得到谋害人命的报酬，

　　因此很快就离开了佛罗伦萨，

决不再回来。——他们顶着血债就此逃亡海外。

60

Yet they contriv'd to steal the basil-pot,

　　And to examine it in secret place:

The thing was vile with green and livid spot,

　　And yet they knew it was Lorenzo's face:

The guerdon of their murder they had got,

　　And so left Florence in a moment's space,

Never to turn again. — Away they went,

With blood upon their heads, to banishment.

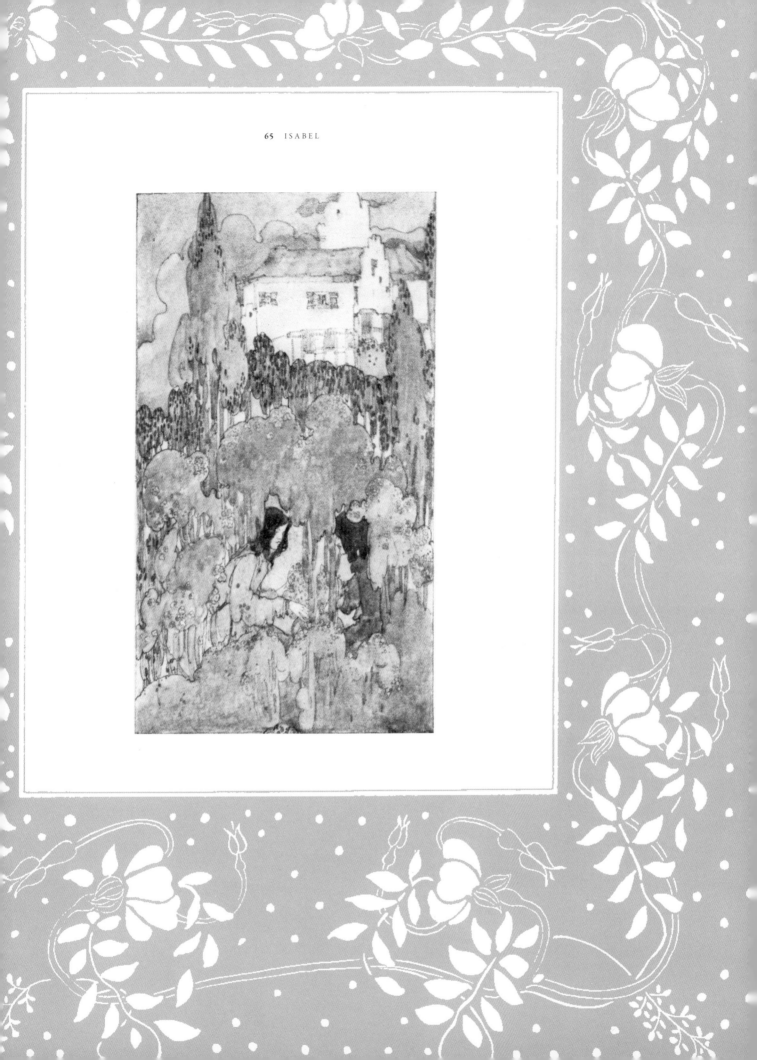

61

"悲哀"啊，移开你的眼睛吧！

　"音乐"呀"音乐"，沮丧地吹奏吧！

"回声"呀"回声"，等到有一天，

　　从默默无闻的岛屿上向我们悲叹吧！

悲痛的众魂啊，不要唱你们的哀歌，

　　因为伊莎贝拉，可爱的伊莎贝拉，

就将死去；就将太孤寂、太遗憾地死去，

因为他们拿走了她美丽的罗勒花。

61

O Melancholy, turn thine eyes away!

　O Music, Music, breathe despondingly!

O Echo, Echo, on some other day,

　　From isles Lethean, sigh to us — O sigh!

Spirits of grief, sing not your "Well-a-way!"

　　For Isabel, sweet Isabel, will die;

Will die a death too lone and incomplete,

Now they have ta'en away her basil sweet.

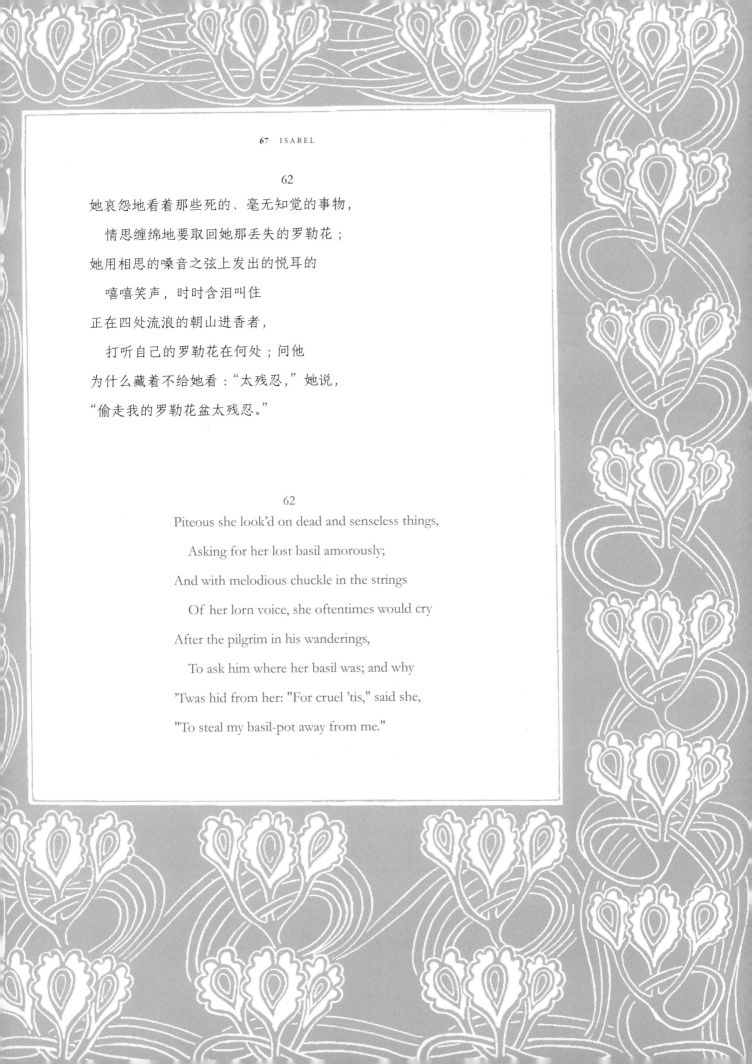

62

她哀怨地看着那些死的、毫无知觉的事物，

　　情思缠绵地要取回她那丢失的罗勒花；

她用相思的嗓音之弦上发出的悦耳的

　　嘻嘻笑声，时时含泪叫住

正在四处流浪的朝山进香者，

　　打听自己的罗勒花在何处；问他

为什么藏着不给她看："太残忍，"她说，

"偷走我的罗勒花盆太残忍。"

62

Piteous she look'd on dead and senseless things,

　　Asking for her lost basil amorously;

And with melodious chuckle in the strings

　　Of her lorn voice, she oftentimes would cry

After the pilgrim in his wanderings,

　　To ask him where her basil was; and why

'Twas hid from her: "For cruel 'tis," said she,

"To steal my basil-pot away from me."

63

她就这么憔悴、这么凄凉地死去，

　　直到最后还在寻找她的罗勒花。

佛罗伦萨城中没有一颗心儿

　　不怀着怜悯悲叹她那忧郁的爱情。

于是关于这故事的一支悲切的歌曲，

　　口口相传，流行于那一带：

这样的叠句仍在被哼唱——"残忍呀，

就这样把我的罗勒花盆偷走！"

63

And so she pined, and so she died forlorn,

　　Imploring for her basil to the last.

No heart was there in Florence but did mourn

　　In pity of her love, so overcast.

And a sad ditty of this story born

　　From mouth to mouth through all the country pass'd:

Still is the burthen sung — "O cruelty,

To steal my basil-pot away from me!"

图书在版编目（CIP）数据

伊沙贝拉：插图珍藏版 /（英）约翰·济慈著；
（英）威廉·布朗·麦克杜格尔绘；朱维基译 . —— 南京：
江苏凤凰文艺出版社，2022.12 （2023.3 重印）

ISBN 978-7-5594-6519-1

Ⅰ . ①伊… Ⅱ . ①约… ②威… ③朱… Ⅲ . ①诗歌 –
英国 – 近代 Ⅳ . ① I561.24

中国版本图书馆 CIP 数据核字 (2022) 第 158781 号

伊莎贝拉（插图珍藏版）

[英] 约翰·济慈 著　　[英] 威廉·布朗·麦克杜格尔 绘　　朱维基 译

策　　划　　尚　飞

责任编辑　　曹　波

特约编辑　　毛菊丹

装帧设计　　墨白空间·李　易

出版发行　　江苏凤凰文艺出版社

　　　　　　南京市中央路 165 号，邮编：210009

网　　址　　http://www.jswenyi.com

印　　刷　　天津图文方嘉印刷有限公司

开　　本　　889 毫米 ×1194 毫米　1/16

印　　张　　4.5

字　　数　　15 千字

版　　次　　2022 年 12 月第 1 版

印　　次　　2023 年 3 月第 2 次印刷

书　　号　　ISBN 978-7-5594-6519-1

定　　价　　98.00 元

江苏凤凰文艺版图书凡印刷、装订错误，可向出版社调换，联系电话 025 – 83280257